I SURVIVED

THE SINKING OF THE *TITANIC*, 1912

I SURVIVED

THE SINKING OF THE *TITANIC*, 1912

THE SHARK ATTACKS OF 1916

I SURVIVED

THE SINKING OF THE *TITANIC*, 1912

by **Lauren Tarshis**

illustrated by **Scott Dawson**

Scholastic Inc.

NEW YORK   TORONTO   LONDON   AUCKLAND

SYDNEY   MEXICO CITY   NEW DELHI   HONG KONG

Text copyright © 2010 by Lauren Tarshis
Illustrations copyright © 2010 by Scholastic Inc.
All rights reserved. Published by Scholastic Inc.
SCHOLASTIC and associated logos are trademarks
and/or registered trademarks of Scholastic Inc.

ISBN 978-93-5275-681-0

First printing, June 2010
This edition: June 2022
Designed by Tim Hall
Printed in India

FOR DAVID

ACKNOWLEDGMENTS

I'd like to thank my agent, Gail Hochman, for all she did to bring this series to life. I am also grateful to my wonderful editor at Scholastic, Amanda Maciel, and to Ellie Berger and Debra Dorfman, for welcoming me to the world of Scholastic books. Ben Kanter and Aaron Leopold helped me get this right. And to my children, Leo, Jeremy, Dylan, and Valerie, who make every day a thrilling journey.

The statistics and facts in this book were drawn mainly from two sources: *A Night to Remember*, by Walter Lord (Henry Holt, 1955) and *Titanic: The Ship Magnificent*, Volumes I and II, by Bruce Beveridge, Scott Andrews, Steve Hall, and Daniel Kistorner (The History Press Ltd., 2008).

CHAPTER 1

MONDAY, APRIL 15, 1912

2:00 A.M.

ON THE DECK OF RMS *TITANIC*

The *Titanic* was sinking.

The gigantic ship had hit an iceberg.

Land was far, far away.

Ten-year-old George Calder stood on the deck.

He shivered because the night was freezing cold.

And because he was scared. More scared than he'd ever been before.

More scared than when Papa swore he'd send George to the army school, far from everything and everyone.

More scared, even, than the time the black panther chased him through the woods back home in Millerstown, New York.

The deck of the *Titanic* was packed with people. Some were running and shouting.

"Help us!"

"Take my baby!"

"Jump!"

Some just plain screamed. Children cried. A gunshot exploded across the deck. But George didn't move.

Just hold on, he told himself, gripping the rail. Like maybe he could hold up the ship.

He couldn't look down at that black water. He kept his eyes on the sky. He had never seen so many stars. Papa said that Mama watched over him from heaven.

Could Mama see him now?

The ship lurched.

"We're going down!" a man shouted.

George closed his eyes, praying this was all a dream.

Even more terrible sounds filled the air. Glass shattering. Furniture crashing. More screams and cries. A bellowing sound, like a giant beast was dying a terrible death. George tried to hold the rail. But he lost his grip. He tumbled, smashing his head on the deck.

And then George couldn't see anything.

Even the stars above him seemed to go black.

CHAPTER 2

19 HOURS EARLIER . . .
SUNDAY, APRIL 14, 1912
7:15 A.M.
FIRST CLASS SUITE, B DECK, RMS *TITANIC*

George woke up early that morning, half expecting to hear Papa calling him for chores.

But then he remembered: the *Titanic*!

He was on the greatest ship in the world.

It was their fifth day at sea. George and his

eight-year-old sister, Phoebe, had spent two months in England with their aunt Daisy. What a time they had! As a surprise for George's tenth birthday, Aunt Daisy took them to see the Tower of London, where they used to chop off your head if the king didn't like you.

Now they were heading back to America.

Back to Papa and their little farm in upstate New York.

George got out of bed and knelt by the small, round window that looked out on the ocean.

"Morning," said Phoebe, peering through the silk curtains of her bed and fumbling for her spectacles. Her curly brown hair was practically standing straight up. "What were you looking for?"

George had to smile. Phoebe always had a question, even at the crack of dawn.

Maybe that's why she was the smartest little sister in the world.

"I thought I saw a giant squid," George said. "And it's coming to get us!"

George rushed over and grabbed Phoebe with wiggly squid arms. She curled up into a ball and laughed.

She was still laughing when Aunt Daisy came in. Even in her robe and slippers, Aunt Daisy was the prettiest lady on the whole ship. Sometimes George couldn't believe she was so old: twenty-two!

"What's this?" Aunt Daisy said. "You know the rule: No having fun without me!"

Phoebe sat up and put her arms around George. "Georgie said he saw a giant squid."

Aunt Daisy laughed. "I wouldn't doubt it. Everyone wants to get a look at the *Titanic*. Even sea monsters."

George halfway believed it. He'd never imagined anything like the *Titanic*.

Aunt Daisy called the ship a floating palace. But it was way better than the cold and dusty castles they'd seen in England. They had three whole rooms—one for Phoebe and George, one for Aunt Daisy, and one for sitting around and doing nothing. They even had a man, a steward named Henry. He had bright red hair and an Irish accent that made everything he said sound like a jolly song.

"Some fresh towels for your bath?" he would say. "Some cocoa before bed?"

And just before they turned out the lights for the night, Henry would knock on their door and peep his head in.

"Is there anything else you might need?" he'd ask.

George kept trying to think of *something* he needed.

But what could you ever need on the *Titanic*?

The ship had everything, even a swimming pool with ocean water heated up like a bath, even gold silk curtains for your bed so you could pretend you were sleeping in a pirate's den, even three dining rooms where you could eat anything you wanted. Last night George had eaten two plates of roast beef, veal and ham pie, carrots sweet as candy, and a mysterious dessert called meringue pudding. It tasted like sugary clouds.

Actually, there *was* one thing missing from the *Titanic*: the New York Giants baseball team. George wondered what Henry would say if George said, "I need shortstop Artie Fletcher right away!"

Probably Henry would say, "Coming right up, sir!"

George grinned just thinking about it.

But Aunt Daisy wasn't smiling at him. She looked very serious.

"We have to make the most of our last three days at sea," Aunt Daisy said in a low voice. "I want you to promise me, George. *No more* trouble!"

George gulped.

Was she really still mad at him for last night?

He'd slid down the banister of the grand staircase in the first class lobby. How could he

resist? The wood was so shiny and polished, curving around like a ride at the fair.

"That lady could have moved out of the way," George said.

"How could she?" Phoebe said. "She was wearing a hundred pounds of diamonds!"

Aunt Daisy almost smiled. George could tell.

No, she could never stay mad at George for long.

Aunt Daisy put her face very close to George's. She had freckles on her nose, just like George and Phoebe.

"No more trouble," she repeated, tapping his chest. "I don't want to have to send a telegram to your father."

George's stomach tightened into a baseball.

"Don't tell Papa!" Phoebe said. "He'll send George away to that army school!"

"I'll be good," George promised. "I will, really."

"You better be," Aunt Daisy said.

CHAPTER 3

George didn't mean to get into trouble.

It's just that he got these *great* ideas.

Like on their first day at sea, when he had climbed up the huge ladder into the crow's nest.

"Aunt Daisy!" he'd yelled, waving his arms.

She had looked up. And she'd almost fainted.

And yesterday George had explored the entire ship. Aunt Daisy kept warning him that he'd get lost. She said the ship was like a maze. But George could always find his way. Even in the huge forest that stretched out behind their farm. Mama used to say that George had a map of the world behind his eyes.

He saw the engine rooms and the boiler rooms, and wound up on the third-class recreation deck. He was watching some boys play marbles when he noticed that he wasn't alone. A little boy was staring up at him with huge eyes the color of amber glass.

"See," the boy said. "See."

And he held out a postcard of the Statue of Liberty. He looked so proud, like he'd carved that big lady himself. George felt like he had to show something in return, so he took out his good-luck charm, the bowie knife Papa had given him for his ninth birthday. He let the little boy run his fingers across the handle, which was carved from an elk's antler.

"Enzo," the little boy said, puffing out his chest and pointing to himself.

"George," said George.

"Giorgio!" the little boy cried with a smile.

A man sitting near them laughed. He was reading an Italian-English dictionary and had the same huge eyes as the boy. George guessed right that he was Enzo's father.

"Marco," he said, shaking George's hand. "You are our first American friend."

Marco must have been studying that dictionary pretty hard, because George understood everything he said. George learned that Enzo was four years old. He'd lost his mama too. He and Marco came from a little town in Italy, and now they were moving to New York City. George told Marco about their farm and their trip and explained that any decent person living in New York had to be a Giants fan. For some reason, Marco thought that was funny.

When it was time for George to leave, Enzo got upset. Very upset.

"Giorgio!" he howled, loud enough for the entire ship to hear.

People stared and put their hands over their ears. Marco promised that they'd see George again, but Enzo wouldn't quit howling. George had never heard anything so loud.

By the time Enzo let go of George's leg and George ran back up to the suite, Aunt Daisy was practically howling too.

"I thought you fell overboard!" she cried.

But even then she wasn't really mad.

She didn't get *really* mad until last night.

How that lady screamed when George came sliding down the banister—like he really was a giant squid.

George didn't mind getting yelled at. He was used to it. Not a day at school went by without Mr. Landers shouting "George! Settle down!" And Papa, well, he always seemed to be mad at George.

But not Aunt Daisy. And being on this trip was supposed to make her happy, happy for the first time since her husband died last year. It had been Uncle Cliff's dream to be on the maiden voyage of the *Titanic*. He'd struck it rich selling automobiles and had plenty of money to pay for one of the biggest suites on the ship.

When Uncle Cliff had his accident, George was sure Aunt Daisy would cancel the trip. Instead she'd invited George and Phoebe to go with her.

And to George's shock, Papa said they could.

"Your aunt's going on this trip to find a little peace," he'd said to George. "I expect you to be a perfect gentleman."

And if he wasn't, George knew he'd be shipped off to that army school for sure. Papa had been talking about that place ever since George had brought the two-foot rat snake to school to show Mr. Landers—because they were studying reptiles!

George had been perfect the whole time in England. He'd let Aunt Daisy drag him to a fancy clothes store for a new pair of boots. He even learned to drink tea without spitting it back into the cup.

But, well, the *Titanic*.

The ship gave him so many great ideas!

But now he'd really be perfect.

No more ideas for the rest of the voyage.

CHAPTER 4

Phoebe wasn't taking any chances with George.

"I'm not letting you out of my sight," she announced after they'd finished breakfast. "I'm your guardian angel."

"I didn't know angels wore spectacles," he said, tugging on one of Phoebe's curls.

"The smart ones do," Phoebe said, grabbing George's arm. She offered him a lemon drop from the little silver tin she'd been carrying around since London.

George made a face. He hated those old-lady candies.

George wanted to go find Marco and Enzo and hear more about Italy. He wanted to ride the elevators up and down. Hardly any other ship in the world had elevators! Better yet, he wanted to find Mr. Andrews, the ship's designer.

When Mr. Andrews had stopped by their table at dinner the first night, George thought he was just another boring millionaire coming over to kiss Aunt Daisy's hand.

But Mr. Andrews was different.

"You *built* the *Titanic?*" said George.

Mr. Andrews smiled. "Not by myself. It took thousands of men to build her. But I did design her, that's true."

He invited George and Phoebe to come with him to the first class writing room. He unrolled the ship's blueprints across a long, polished table.

It was like looking at the skeleton of a giant beast.

"She's the biggest moving object ever built," Mr. Andrews explained. "Fourteen stories tall. Forty-five thousand tons of steel. And longer than four city blocks."

"Our aunt says nothing bad can happen to this ship," Phoebe said. "People say it's unsinkable."

"No ship is safer," Mr. Andrews said. "That is certainly true."

"What if the *Titanic* was hit by a meteor?" said Phoebe, whose latest obsession was outer space. She was determined to see a shooting star before they docked in New York.

Mr. Andrews didn't laugh or roll his eyes like Mr. Landers did when Phoebe asked her questions.

"I hadn't planned on any meteors hitting the ship," Mr. Andrews said thoughtfully. "But I'd like to think she could take almost anything and still float."

Phoebe seemed satisfied.

"Are there any secret passages?" said George.

19

Mr. Andrews studied his blueprints, and then pointed to the boiler rooms.

"There are escape ladders," he said. "They run up the starboard side of the ship, up two decks, through the stokers' quarters, and into their dining hall. I hear the crew likes using them instead of the stairs."

George could have stayed there all night. He

asked a million questions and Mr. Andrews answered every single one.

"I was like you when I was a boy," Mr. Andrews said just before Aunt Daisy came to haul George off to bed. "One day I predict you'll build a ship of your own."

George knew that would never happen. He could barely get through a day at school. But he liked that Mr. Andrews said it. And he sure wanted to find those secret ladders.

But Phoebe had different ideas.

First she dragged George to the first class library so she could check out a book on Halley's comet. Then she took him on a walk on the boat deck. He felt like a dog.

"Strange," Phoebe said, looking at the lifeboats that hung just off the deck. "There are only sixteen boats. That's not nearly enough for everyone."

"The ship's unsinkable," George said. "So do we really need lifeboats at all?"

Phoebe stared at the boats and shrugged. "I guess you're right," she said. And then she announced that it was time to see how many ladies were wearing hats with blue feathers.

George groaned.

This would be the most boring day of his life.

But at least nobody was yelling at him.

CHAPTER 5

At dinner that night, Aunt Daisy raised her glass. "To George! No trouble for one entire day!"

They clinked their glasses together just as an old man stopped by their table.

"Mrs. Key," the man said to Aunt Daisy. "I've been meaning to say hello."

"Mr. Stead!" Aunt Daisy said. "What a pleasure. This is George, my nephew, and Phoebe, my niece."

Mr. Stead nodded hello.

"So," Aunt Daisy said. "What brings you onto this magnificent ship?"

"Oh, I couldn't miss it," he said. "I think all of society is on this ship. I hear there's even an Egyptian princess on board."

"Really!" Aunt Daisy said. "I haven't met her!"

"Well, none of us have. She's traveling in the first class baggage room."

"Excuse me?" Aunt Daisy said.

"The princess is more than twenty-five hundred years old," Mr. Stead said.

George's ears perked up.

"I'm not sure I understand," Aunt Daisy said.

"She's a mummy," Mr. Stead said.

"A mummy!" Phoebe gasped.

"That's right," Mr. Stead said. "From a tomb near Thebes. I understand she belongs to a man named Mr. Burrows. People are saying he sold the coffin to the British Museum. Then he packed the princess herself in a wooden crate. Apparently

24

he's bringing her back for his collection. Some say it's bad luck to take a mummy from its tomb."

"I'm glad I'm not the superstitious type!" Aunt Daisy said.

Mr. Stead chuckled. "In any case, nothing can harm this ship. Not even the curse of a mummy!"

Mr. Stead tipped his hat and said good-bye.

"Mr. Stead is a very famous writer in England," Aunt Daisy said. "You never know who you'll meet on the *Titanic*!"

And then it hit George, the best idea ever.

That mummy! He had to see it.

Maybe this day wasn't so boring after all.

CHAPTER 6

George didn't tell Phoebe or Aunt Daisy about his plan.

He figured he'd head down to the first class baggage room after they went to sleep. He'd find Mr. Burrows's crate, pry it open, and take a quick peek at the mummy. He'd be back in bed and snoring away before anyone knew he was gone.

It was almost eleven-fifteen when Phoebe was

finally asleep and the light was out under Aunt Daisy's door. George crept out of bed. He quickly got dressed and put his knife in his pocket. He'd need it for prying off the lid of the crate. And who knew? Maybe there was a live cobra in the box too. George could hope, couldn't he?

George opened the door and peeked into the hallway. He wanted to avoid Henry, who seemed to have eyes in the back of his bright orange head. He wouldn't like George creeping around so late at night.

But the hallway was quiet. There was no noise at all except for the quiet hum of the engines, rising up from the bottom of the ship. George loved that noise. It made him think of crickets in the woods at night.

In fact, being out here all by himself reminded him of the nights at home when he sneaked out into the woods while Papa and Phoebe were asleep.

He'd head out when his mind was filled with restless thoughts.

About why Papa was always mad at him, or why he didn't try harder in school.

And of course Mama.

Almost three years had passed since she died. George tried not to think about her too much. But some nights when he closed his eyes, he'd remember her smile. Or her smell when she hugged him close. Like fresh grass and sweet flowers.

And that song she'd sing to wake George up in the morning:

"Awake, awake.
It's now daybreak!
But don't forget your dreams. . . ."

Thinking about Mama was like standing close to a fire. Warm at first. But get too close and it hurt too much.

Much better to stay clear of those thoughts.

Nothing cleared George's mind quicker than being in the woods. He never stayed out for more than an hour or two. . . . Except for that night back in October.

George was heading back toward home when he heard a terrible sound, like a little girl screaming. He turned around, and in the dark distance he saw two glowing yellow eyes.

Some old-timers said there were black panthers in the woods, but George never believed it.

But as the yellow eyes got closer, George could see the outline of a huge cat, with two glistening fangs.

George told himself not to run. He knew he'd never outrun the panther.

But he couldn't help it—he ran as fast as he could. Branches cut his face, but he didn't slow down.

Any second the panther would leap up and tackle George. Its claws would tear him apart.

George could feel the cat right behind him; he could smell its breath, like rotting meat. George grabbed a fallen branch. He turned and waved it in front of him. The panther lunged and grabbed the branch in its jaws.

George let go of the stick and scrambled up a tree, climbing as high as he could go.

The cat dropped the branch and came after him, like a shadow with glowing eyes.

George pulled out his knife.

He waited until the cat's front paws were on the small branch just below him. And then, with all his might, he chopped at the branch with his knife.

Crack.

The branch broke free.

The giant cat tumbled through the air, screaming and crashing through the branches, and then hit the ground with a thud.

There was silence.

And then the cat stood up. It looked up at George for a long moment.

And it turned and walked slowly back into the woods.

George stayed in the tree until it was just about light, and made it into bed just before Papa woke up.

His friends at school refused to believe George when he told them, even when he swore on his heart.

"No way."

"Big fat lie."

"Next thing you'll be saying is that you've been signed by the Giants." Their laughter rose up around George, but it didn't bother him, because right then he realized that it didn't matter what they thought.

George knew he'd faced down the panther.

And he'd never forget it.

CHAPTER 7

Just thinking about seeing the mummy made George happy. He went down five flights of stairs to G deck and practically skipped along the long hallway toward the front of the ship. He ducked into doorways a few times to hide from the night stewards. But he had no trouble finding his way, not like Phoebe, who got lost walking from the dining room to the washroom.

"Next time I'll leave a trail of bread crumbs,

like Hansel and Gretel," she'd said, their first day on board.

"How about lemon drops?" George had suggested.

Phoebe had giggled.

The hold was in the very front of the ship, past the mail sorting room and the cabins where the stokers and firemen stayed. Too bad, George thought, that there wasn't time to sneak in and see the escape ladders. Luckily there were two more days at sea.

George walked right through the doors of the first class baggage room and down a steep metal staircase that led to the hold. All around him were crates and trunks and bags neatly stacked on shelves and lined up on the floor.

It took him a minute to figure out that everything was arranged in alphabetical order, by the owners' names, and a few minutes to find the *B*s.

And there it was, a plain wooden crate stamped with the words:

MR. DAVID BURROWS
NEW YORK CITY
CONTENTS FRAGILE

George smiled to himself.

This was going to be easy.

He took out his knife and started to pry off the lid. He worked carefully, prying each nail loose so he'd be able to close the crate tight again when he was finished.

He'd made it halfway around when he heard a strange sound.

The hair on his arms prickled.

It was the same feeling he'd had the night of the panther, that someone — or something — was watching him.

George stared at the crate, his heart pounding.

And before he could even take a breath, something leaped out of the shadows and pushed him to the ground.

George looked up, half expecting to see a mummy rising out of the crate, her arms reaching for George's throat.

What he saw was almost as horrifying.

It was a man with glittering blue eyes and a scar running down the side of his face.

He grabbed George's knife out of his hand. The man was small, but very strong.

"I'll take this," he said, admiring it. Then he looked George up and down.

"So," the man said. "Trying to fill your pockets with some first class loot?"

George realized he must be a robber. George had caught him in the act!

"Uh, no, I'm . . ."

The man pointed to George's boots. "Which trunk did you steal those from? Cost more than a third class ticket, I'd say."

George shook his head. "I got them in London," he said, and too late realized he'd made a mistake.

"Ah, a prince from first class," the man said with a hearty laugh. "Just down here for a little thrill? What's your name?"

"George," said George softly.

"Prince George," the man said, bowing in a joking way. "A pity those boots wouldn't fit me," he added, standing up. "But you do have something I'd like. Your key. Always wanted to see one of those first class cabins."

There was no way George could let this man up to the suite! He'd jump overboard before he let him near Aunt Daisy and Phoebe.

"There's a mummy down here!" he blurted out. "It's worth millions! It's in that crate!"

The man raised an eyebrow.

George kept talking.

"I thought I could sneak it off the ship and sell it in New York," George lied. "My father's business is bad. I thought if I could sell it . . ."

The man looked at the crate.

"I like the way you think," he said.

He waved the knife at George and told him not to move. And then he quickly worked the knife around the lid. Obviously he'd done this many times before.

He lifted the lid off the crate. But before either of them could look inside, there was a tremendous rumbling noise, and the entire hold began to shake so hard that George almost fell. The shaking got stronger and stronger, the noise louder and louder, like thunder exploding all around them. A trunk tumbled off a shelf and hit the scar-faced man on the head. The knife clattered to the floor, but George didn't try to get it. Here was his chance to escape. He spun around, ran up the stairs, and darted out the door.

CHAPTER 8

George ran as fast as he could down the hall. He heard shouting behind him, but he didn't stop until he was back on B deck, safe again in first class.

A steward hurried past him with a stack of clean towels.

"Good evening, sir," he said.

George nodded, out of breath.

Nothing could happen to him up here, he knew. So why was his heart still pounding?

It was the ship, he realized—that thundering noise. That shaking in the hold. Had a boiler exploded? Had a steam pipe burst?

An eerie silence surrounded him, and George's heart skipped a beat as he realized that the engines had been turned off. The quiet rumbling had stopped.

Just outside, George heard people talking loudly. Did they know what was happening?

George went out onto the deck and walked over to the small crowd of men. Most were still dressed in their dinner tuxedos and puffing on cigars. They were standing at the rail, pointing and laughing at something happening on the well deck, one level below. What was so funny?

George squeezed between two men and looked over the rail.

At first he was sure his eyes were playing tricks. It looked like the well deck had been through a winter storm. It was covered with ice and slush. A bunch of young men in tattered coats and hats were pelting each other with balls of ice, roaring with laughter like kids having a snowball fight.

"What's happened?" asked a man who'd walked up behind George.

"The ship nudged an iceberg!" said an old man with a bushy mustache. He didn't sound worried.

An iceberg!

"Is that why they've stopped the engines?" said the new man. "Because of some ice on the deck?"

"Just being cautious, it seems, following regulations," said the older fellow. "I spoke to one of the officers. He assured me we'll be underway any moment. Hey there!" he yelled down to the young men below. "Toss some of that ice up here!"

One of the gang picked up a piece of ice the size of a baseball. He threw it, but the man with the bushy mustache missed. George reached out and made a clean catch with one hand. The crowd cheered. George held up the ice and smiled. Then he held it out to the man.

"Keep it, son!" he said. "There's plenty for everyone."

The piece of ice was heavier than George had expected.

He sniffed it and wrinkled his nose.

It smelled like old sardines!

More ice balls came sailing up from below, and the men jostled to catch them.

Their laughter and cheers rose up around George, and the fear he'd felt in the baggage hold faded away. From up here, on the deck of this incredible ship, George felt powerful. Nothing could hurt him on the *Titanic*.

Not a meteor falling from space. Not a giant squid.

Not the scar-faced man.

George squinted out into the distance, hoping to see the iceberg, but the sea faded into darkness.

His teeth were chattering now. It was so much

colder than it had been at dinnertime. He wanted to be back in bed, curled up under his fancy first class sheets and blankets.

The corridor was still quiet as George crept toward his suite.

As he was letting himself in, he stepped on something that made a crunching sound under his boot. At first George thought that it was ice or a piece of glass. But when he picked up his heel, he saw that the carpet was covered with yellow crystals.

George smiled. It was just one of Phoebe's lemon drops.

George let himself in, easing the door shut.

Phoebe's bed curtains were closed. The light under Aunt Daisy's door was off.

George quickly changed into his pajamas and climbed into bed.

Yes, he was safe, he told himself.

He tried to go to sleep, but as the minutes ticked by, his mind got restless.

It hit him that his knife was gone, forever, and the total silence of the ship seemed to press down on him. Why hadn't the engines started up again?

He lay wide awake, listening and wondering.

It was almost a relief when he heard someone knocking on their door.

CHAPTER 9

It was Henry.

"Hello, George," said Henry. "Can I speak to Mrs. Key, please?"

Henry wore his usual polite smile, but his voice wasn't jolly.

"What is it?" said Aunt Daisy, stepping out of her room.

"So sorry to barge in like this, ma'am," Henry said. "But there's been an . . . incident."

Aunt Daisy glared at George.

"I'm so sorry, Henry," she said in an exasperated voice. "My nephew here just can't seem to stay out of trouble!"

"Oh, no, ma'am!" Henry exclaimed. "This has nothing to do with George. It's the ship, ma'am. Seems we've bumped an iceberg. I'm sure the captain is just being cautious, but he wants everyone up on deck."

"It's after midnight," Aunt Daisy said with a laugh. "Surely the captain doesn't expect us to appear on deck in our nightclothes!"

"No, ma'am. It's very cold outside." Henry walked over to the dresser and brought out three life jackets. "And you'll need to put these on. Over your coats."

Aunt Daisy stared at the life jackets as if Henry was holding up clown costumes.

"Henry! I'm not taking the children out into the cold for some kind of drill! Has Captain Smith lost his senses?"

"Of course not, Mrs. Key," Henry said. "Now

47

if you could get yourself and the children ready. I'll be back in just a moment to see if you need any help."

He left them alone.

"All right, George," Aunt Daisy said. "I guess we'll have another adventure to boast about when we get back. You get dressed. I'll get Phoebe up."

Aunt Daisy went to Phoebe's bed, pulling aside the curtains.

George heard a gasp, and he rushed over.

Phoebe wasn't there.

"Where could she be?" Aunt Daisy exclaimed.

A cold feeling crept up George's spine. Phoebe, his guardian angel. She must have woken up while George was gone, and now she was somewhere on the ship. Searching for George.

He took a deep breath.

"I went out exploring," George said. "After you went to bed. I didn't think Phoebe would wake up. She never does!"

"So she's out there looking for you?" Aunt Daisy said.

George nodded. "She doesn't want me getting into trouble." He kept his eyes glued to the floor. Aunt Daisy should be furious with him, and Papa was right! George had no sense. Not one lick of sense.

How would they ever find Phoebe?

But then George had an idea . . . that lemon drop in the hallway.

Could it be?

He ran out into the corridor, which was still empty. It seemed Henry wasn't having much luck getting people out of bed and up onto the deck.

George ran a little ways down the hall.

There!

He hurried down a bit farther.

Yes! Another lemon drop!

Phoebe! His smart sister!

Aunt Daisy came up behind him.

"She's left a trail of lemon drops," George said.

Aunt Daisy looked confused.

"Like Hansel and Gretel," George explained. "She left a trail so she could find her way back."

CHAPTER 10

George and Aunt Daisy scrambled to get dressed and put on their life jackets. Aunt Daisy brought Phoebe's warmest coat, and George carried the extra life jacket. They'd quickly find Phoebe and head up to the boat deck. And tomorrow morning this would be a big joke to laugh at over breakfast.

George thought that Phoebe had gone to the promenade deck—that she'd been woken up by the commotion with the ice and figured that George had gone out to see what was happening.

But when they got to the main staircase, he saw that the yellow glints were headed downstairs, not up to the deck.

His heart sank.

Phoebe had headed down to the first class baggage hold. Because she knew that George would want to see that mummy.

Of course she'd known.

Phoebe could read his mind.

A chill went through George's bones.

What if the scar-faced man was lurking in the baggage hold when Phoebe got there?

He ran faster down the stairs now. Aunt Daisy called after him, but he didn't slow down.

But when he got down to G deck, there was a gate stretched across the doorway.

"This wasn't here when I came down," he said to Aunt Daisy. He tried to pull it open, but it was locked. And just on the other side there was

a mob of people standing restlessly, third class passengers from the looks of their worn clothing.

"Look," Aunt Daisy said, pointing at one of Phoebe's candies glinting on the floor on the other side of the gate, pushed next to the wall. "She's down here. Pardon me!" she called to the steward standing in front of the crowd.

"You've gone the wrong way, madam," he said, staring at Aunt Daisy's huge diamond ring. "The captain wants first class passengers up on the boat deck now."

"My niece is down here somewhere," Aunt Daisy said. "You need to let us through."

"I'm sure she wouldn't have wandered down this far," the steward said.

"We're quite sure she's down here," Aunt Daisy said. "So if you'll please open the gate."

"I'm sorry, madam," he said. "Regulations . . ."

"Open this gate at once!" Aunt Daisy shouted in a tone George had never heard her use before.

The man took a key from his pocket and opened the gate. He stepped aside to let them pass. The crowd surged forward.

"Get back!" the steward shouted. "We'll tell you when it's time for you to go up!"

A few of the men lunged toward him.

Aunt Daisy grabbed George's arm.

The steward took a pistol from his pocket. His hand shook as he waved it toward the crowd. George and Aunt Daisy stepped through the gate. The steward slammed it behind them.

They were trapped down there, just like everyone else.

George and Aunt Daisy squeezed through the crowd, weaving around trunks and stepping over sleeping children. There were so many people. If Phoebe's candies were down here, they couldn't see them anymore.

Suddenly something crashed into George from behind. A pair of arms wrapped around his waist so tightly he couldn't breathe.

George's heart stopped — the scar-faced man?

"GIORGIO!" Enzo screamed up at him.

George's eardrums nearly split in two.

Enzo's father hurried over to them. He tried to gently peel Enzo away from George.

But the little boy wouldn't let go.

"NO!" he howled. "NO!"

"Very sorry," Marco said, smiling apologetically at Aunt Daisy, who looked more confused than ever. "We are old friends of Giorgio."

George started to introduce Aunt Daisy, but before he could get three words out, Enzo was dragging him down the hall, elbowing his way through the crowd like a pint-sized bull.

"See! See!" Enzo said.

"What?" George said. "No . . ."

"See! See!"

What was this kid doing? What did he want George to see?

The answer was just a few steps away, through an open doorway.

It was the mail sorting room.

Except now all George could see was water, green water swirling halfway up the stairs, foaming and churning like a stormy river. Sacks of mail bobbed up and down. Hundreds of letters floated on the surface.

And now George understood what Enzo was saying.

Sea.

The sea.

The *Titanic* was filling with water from the sea.

CHAPTER 11

Unsinkable.

Unsinkable.

George whispered those words like a prayer, over and over in his mind. He thought of Mr. Andrews, of how sure he was of this ship.

But the longer he stared at that water, that foaming green water, rising higher every second, the more certain he became: The *Titanic* was in trouble.

"We must go up," Marco said to Aunt Daisy. "We find a way."

But she shook her head, holding up Phoebe's bright blue coat and her life jacket.

"My niece, Phoebe," Aunt Daisy said. "She's down here. . . ."

George could see she was fighting back tears. George had never seen her look so sad and helpless, not even when Uncle Cliff died.

"She came down here looking for me," George said. "We can't find her."

Marco's amber eyes became very intent.

"An idea," he said. He knelt down and spoke to Enzo in Italian.

The boy smiled and nodded.

Then Marco hoisted the little boy up onto his shoulders.

Enzo took a huge breath and screamed,

"Phoebe!

"PHOEBE!"

People stopped talking and stared up at the boy with the foghorn voice.

"Phoebe!

"PHOEBE!"

As a hush fell over the crowd, George heard a faint voice.

"I'm here! I'm here!"

The crowd parted, and Phoebe appeared, her spectacles crooked, her face pale.

She staggered forward and threw her arms around George, burying her face in his chest.

"I found you," she whispered.

George didn't bother arguing over who did the finding. And anyway, his words were stuck in his throat. So he just held her tight.

It took some time for Phoebe to calm down enough to tell her story: that yes, she had been looking for George and heading for the baggage hold, that she got caught in the crowd of people rushing toward the back of the ship.

"It was like a stampede," she said.

As Phoebe talked, Aunt Daisy helped her into her coat and life jacket. Enzo held Phoebe's hand, like they were old friends. And the strange thing was that it felt that way, like they'd known Marco and Enzo forever. Maybe that's what happened when you got trapped in a flooding ship together.

George started to feel calmer with Phoebe close to him.

But then came a deep booming sound, a kind of groaning that echoed up all around them. At first George thought maybe the engines had started up again. But no, this wasn't the sound of the *Titanic*'s mighty engines.

The entire ship catapulted forward. People fell, toppling like dominoes. George was thrown into the wall. Screams and shouts echoed through the hallway. He managed to grab Enzo by the life jacket as he went sailing by him. Enzo just giggled as he fell into George's lap. To him this was a fun game. George hoped he never figured out that it wasn't.

"What was that?" Phoebe gasped, digging her fingers into George's arms.

Nobody answered.

But they all knew.

The *Titanic* was sinking.

"We will go up," Marco said.

"How?" Aunt Daisy said.

Phoebe grabbed George's hand.

"You, Georgie," she said.

"What?" George said.

"Phoebe's right," Aunt Daisy said. "You know the ship better than anyone." She turned to Marco. "He's explored every inch."

George couldn't believe it. They were counting on him?

But what if he made a mistake?

What if they all got lost?

"You can do it," Phoebe whispered.

And so George closed his eyes, picturing Mr. Andrews's blueprints in his mind.

And he remembered: the escape ladders.

He remembered what Mr. Andrews had told him: *The ladders are in the stokers' quarters, and they run up three decks.*

He pointed toward the front of the ship.

"This way," he said.

CHAPTER 12

There was no crowd here. Just abandoned trunks and suitcases.

And water. It was seeping into the hallway from under the doors of some of the cabins. No wonder those people were trying to push their way upstairs. They'd probably known right away that the ship was in trouble and the bottom decks were flooding.

The door to the stokers' quarters was locked.

Marco handed Enzo over to George and rammed the door with his shoulder, breaking the lock.

George rushed inside and went to the back wall.

And there it was, a ladder bolted to the wall. Just like Mr. Andrews said it would be. It came through the floor and shot straight up through an opening in the ceiling. George almost laughed with relief.

"Bravo, George!" Marco said.

"Bravo, Giorgio!" Enzo said, clapping.

George hopped up onto the ladder, with Phoebe and Aunt Daisy at his heels.

George was worried about Enzo, but the little guy scrambled like a monkey right ahead of Marco. They came up in a small dining room meant for crew members, and then George led everyone down a long second class corridor, up the grand staircase, and finally out onto the crowded boat deck.

They'd made it!

An officer came hurrying over to Aunt Daisy.

"Madam, there is a lifeboat about to leave. You and the children must come at once."

The man looked at Marco.

"Women and children only, sir," he said somberly. "I'm afraid you will have to stay with the other gentlemen."

Marco nodded. "Yes," he said. "I know."

Phoebe had been right. There weren't enough lifeboats. Not nearly enough.

What would happen to all of these men on deck? There were hundreds of them! And what about the crew? And those people down on G deck?

George's heart was pounding so hard he thought it would break through his chest.

He felt dizzy and sick.

Marco got down on his knees and spoke very quietly to Enzo.

Enzo nodded. Marco kissed him on the forehead, and then Enzo ran over to Aunt Daisy. She picked him up.

"I say he will go on a special boat ride," Marco said. "I say you will not leave him."

Aunt Daisy nodded, her eyes welling with tears.

"I promise you that."

Marco and Aunt Daisy looked at each other. Neither of them said a word, but a whole conversation seemed to happen with their eyes.

Phoebe was really crying now, looking away so Enzo wouldn't see. George felt like someone was choking him.

"Come on now!" the officer screamed.

And so they left Marco, and when George turned around just a few seconds later, he was gone.

The officer led them through a crowd of men to the side of the ship, where a lifeboat hung just over the side. It was packed with people, all women and children except for two sailors who stood at either end.

An officer helped Phoebe over the rail, and then one of the sailors reached over and pulled her into the boat. George helped Enzo, who tumbled in next to Phoebe. Aunt Daisy had a hard time climbing over in her skirts, but George held her hand, and she finally made it.

Now it was George's turn. As he took a step over the railing, someone pulled him back roughly.

"No more room," the officer said. "Women and children only. Lower away!" he called.

"No!" called Aunt Daisy, standing up in the boat. "He's only ten years old! Wait!"

The lifeboat rocked and almost tipped over. Ladies shrieked.

"You will drown us all!" a woman shouted.

"Sit down or I'll throw you over!" the sailor said.

And now Phoebe was screaming too.

Enzo howled.

George was too shocked to move.

Phoebe leaped up and grabbed hold of one of the ropes. She was trying to climb out of the lifeboat, back to George. He gasped as her hand slipped and she dangled over the sea. A sailor grabbed her around the waist and threw her into the boat.

And then the boat slid down on its ropes and splashed into the water.

Aunt Daisy and Phoebe were shouting up at him as the sailors rowed the boat away. George stood there at the rail, watching, his entire body shaking.

He stood there for what felt like a long time after their boat disappeared into the darkness.

He couldn't look down at the water, so he stared up at the sky, at all of those stars.

He closed his eyes and told himself it was a nightmare. He was really asleep in his suite. Or no, he was home on the farm, in his bed, with

Phoebe sleeping across the room and Papa sitting by the fire downstairs.

He closed his eyes tighter.

He tried to block out the terrible noises around him. He felt himself tipping to the side and he held tighter to the rail. And then he couldn't hold on anymore. His hand slipped.

And George fell, smashing his head on the deck.

And then there was silence.

CHAPTER 13

Strong arms lifted George up. He felt himself being carried.

"Papa?" he said. "Papa?"

Why did his head hurt so much? Had the panther knocked him out of the tree? Was he sick with a fever like Mama? And whose voice was whispering in his ear?

"Giorgio. Giorgio. Wake up."

George opened his eyes. Marco's amber eyes shone down on him.

This was no dream. He was not sick.

The *Titanic* was sinking.

The bow was completely underwater now, and waves swept over the deck. Lounge chairs sailed past them and crashed over the side. People clung to the rails. A few slipped and were swept overboard.

Marco had wrapped one arm around the railing and the other around George.

"It's time to go," Marco said.

"Go where?" George said, even though he knew.

They were going into the water. There was nowhere else for them to go.

Marco held George's arm as they climbed over the railing.

"When we jump, jump as far out as you can," Marco said. "Away from the ship."

George filled his lungs with the icy air.

"Jump!" Marco cried.

George pushed with his feet and leaped off the

boat. He closed his eyes, imagining that he had enormous wings that would take him soaring into the sky.

But then he hit the water, and down he went.

And just when he was sure his lungs would pop, the ocean seemed to spit him back up. George sputtered. The water was so cold it felt like millions of needles were stabbing him. It hurt so much he couldn't move.

Someone grabbed him by the life jacket and started dragging him away from the ship. It took George a few seconds to realize that it was Marco. He stopped to grab a door that was floating by. After helping George climb up on top, Marco found a crate for himself. It wasn't big enough to keep his feet out of the water. But it was better than nothing. The crate had a rope attached to it. Marco tied it around his arm and handed the end to George.

"Hold tight," he said.

They turned and stared at the ship.

The entire front was underwater, and the back had risen toward the sky. It groaned and squeaked and sparked. Black smoke poured from its funnels, and the lights flickered. It was like watching a fairy-tale dragon, stabbed and bleeding, fighting for its life.

And finally it seemed to give up.

The groaning stopped. The lights went dark. And the *Titanic* sank into the bubbling black water, down, down, down, down, until George closed his eyes.

He couldn't make himself watch Mr. Andrews's beautiful ship disappear.

A sound rose up around him, people calling for help. More and more people, screaming and yelling, hundreds of voices swirling together like a howling wind.

Marco pulled George away from the people and the wreckage. George couldn't believe how

strong he was, how hard he kicked, how his arms sliced through the water.

When he finally stopped, Marco was gasping for breath, exhaling cold clouds of white mist. He tightened the rope around his arm and patted George on the shoulder.

"I rest now, Giorgio," he said breathlessly. He closed his eyes and put his head down on the crate. "Soon."

Soon what? George was afraid to ask. Soon it would be over? Soon they would be rescued? Or soon they would be swallowed up by the darkness?

George heard men talking somewhere close by.

He looked around, relieved that he wasn't all by himself, and to his shock, just ahead, he saw a lifeboat.

"Marco!" he said. "Wake up!"

But Marco didn't move. His arms hung off the side of the crate. His feet dangled in the icy water.

"Marco! We need to get to that boat!"

But Marco was still. And George realized that his friend had used every last ounce of strength. He'd gotten George off the sinking ship, and across the icy waters.

It was up to George now.

He tucked the rope under his body and started paddling. The water seared his hands and arms. It was so cold it felt boiling hot, like lava.

But he didn't stop until he reached the boat.

It wasn't a regular wooden lifeboat. It was much smaller, and made of canvas cloth. There were about ten people crowded inside, mostly men. They all seemed dazed and frozen. Nobody spoke as George paddled up and grabbed hold of the side.

But somebody pushed his hand off.

"Get back," a voice said weakly. "You'll put us all in the water."

"Please," George said. "We need help."

George put his hand up again, but again someone pushed it off.

And so George pulled Marco to the other side of the boat. He tried again.

Nobody helped him. But this time nobody stopped him.

It took him three tries, but he managed to hoist himself over the side and tumble into the boat.

And now for Marco.

He got up on his knees and leaned over, bracing his legs against the side of the boat as he grabbed Marco under the arms. He pulled, but Marco was attached to the crate by the rope. He tried again, yanking the rope, digging at the knot with his frozen fingers. But the knot was like rusted metal. George struggled, and water sloshed over the side of the boat.

"Just let him go," one of the men said weakly. "It's hopeless."

But George kept working on the rope, trying now to break it away from the crate. He was pulling so hard that at first he didn't notice that Marco was slipping into the sea.

"Please! Somebody!" George screamed. "Can't you help us?"

A woman from the front of the boat climbed back to George.

She wore a black coat, her head and face hidden by a flowered shawl. As she pushed George aside she pulled something out of her coat.

A knife!

With a clean cut, she sliced the rope and helped George pull Marco into the boat.

Her hands looked surprisingly strong.

George fell back, exhausted.

"Thank you," George said to the woman through his chattering teeth.

The woman didn't say anything, and suddenly George noticed the knife. A bowie knife with an elk-horn handle.

George looked up, under the shawl. Two glittering blue eyes looked back at him.

The scar-faced man.

He had saved Marco's life.

Without a word, he handed George his knife.

Then he looked away.

CHAPTER 14

The cold pressed down on George until it seemed to crush his bones. He huddled close to Marco, trying to keep them both warm. Marco barely moved.

Some of the men sang softly.

Others prayed.

Some made no sounds at all.

Hours went by.

The sea became rougher, and every few minutes a wave splashed into the boat.

George was drifting off to sleep when one of the men shouted.

"It's a ship!"

And sure enough, a bright light was heading toward them.

"No," another man said. "It's just lightning."

But the light was getting bigger. And brighter.

George stared at that light, afraid that if he even blinked it would disappear, but soon he could see the outline of a gigantic ship steaming toward them.

He whispered to Marco, who barely fluttered his eyes. He pulled his friend closer, rubbing his arms.

"It won't be long," he whispered. "Hang on."

As the sky brightened, George gaped at the scene around him. It was as if they'd fallen through a hole in the ocean and come out on the other side of the earth.

There were icebergs all around them— hundreds of them, as far as George could see.

They sparkled in the golden pink light. They were so beautiful, but looking at them sent a chill up George's spine.

As the ship got closer, George could see that it was a passenger steamer, like the *Titanic*. Closer and closer it came, until George could read its name: *Carpathia*.

There were people crowded on the deck, looking over the rail. They were yelling and shouting and waving. But one voice rose above all the others, like a siren:

"PAPA! PAPA! GIORGIO!"

Marco's eyes fluttered, and he smiled a little.

"Enzo," he whispered.

George could see the little boy, waving frantically from Aunt Daisy's arms. Phoebe stood next to them, waving, with the sunlight glinting off her spectacles.

"They're safe, Marco!" George said. "They made it!"

George grabbed Marco's hand.

"And so did we."

CHAPTER 15

Those first two days on the *Carpathia* were a blur.

George mostly slept, on a bed of blankets and pillows on the floor of the first class lounge. But he sensed that Phoebe and Aunt Daisy never left his side. He sometimes heard Enzo singing softly to him in Italian, his breath hot on George's cheek. He heard Aunt Daisy and Phoebe talking—about Marco, whose feet were badly frozen, about the *Carpathia*'s passengers, who couldn't do enough for them all. About the hundreds and hundreds of people who didn't make it out of the water.

Slowly George felt stronger, and on their last night at sea, he was able to go out onto the deck with Phoebe.

They sat on a bench, wrapped in a blanket. A stewardess came over and gave them each a mug of warm milk.

Phoebe looked up at the sky as she warmed her hands on her mug.

"I finally saw a shooting star, when I was on the lifeboat," she said. "You can guess what I wished for."

George reached for her hand.

Yes, of course he knew.

On the bench next to them sat two women. Both were crying. Probably they'd lost their husbands. Or brothers. Or fathers.

There hadn't been enough wishing stars for everyone that night.

Phoebe said that only about 700 of them made it out of the water.

Phoebe leaned in close to George. Her coat smelled like rose water. A lady from the *Carpathia* had given it to her.

"Have you wondered?" she asked quietly, "if maybe there really was a curse?"

At first George didn't understand that Phoebe was talking about the mummy.

With all that had happened, George hadn't thought about it.

But now it hit him: how strange it was that the ship had collided with the iceberg at the exact moment the scar-faced man had opened the lid of Mr. Burrows's crate.

"I guess we'll never know," George said.

But the next evening, as the *Carpathia* was closing in on New York Harbor, George and Phoebe overheard a skinny man with a beard speaking to an officer.

"Before the *Titanic*, I was traveling in Egypt, a

place called Thebes," the man said. "I explored a magnificent tomb of a royal family."

Phoebe's eyes bugged out.

And before George could stop her, she had marched over to the man.

"Excuse me," she said. "Are you Mr. Burrows?"

"Yes, I am," the man replied.

Phoebe took a big breath.

"Mr. Burrows," she said. "This might sound like a very strange question. But did you bring a mummy on board the *Titanic*?"

The man looked at Phoebe.

"A mummy?" he said.

"Yes," she said. "We heard it was a princess."

Mr. Burrows's eyes were tired and sad.

But he smiled a little.

"My princess," he said. "Yes."

"So there *was* a mummy?" Phoebe exclaimed.

"No, child," he said. "One should never take a mummy from a tomb. That is very bad luck.

Princess was my cat. She passed away on my trip to Egypt. And so I had her . . . wrapped, so I could bring her back with me."

"So the princess was a cat?"

"Yes," he said sadly. "The most beautiful cat that ever lived."

Three hours later, just after nine o'clock, the *Carpathia* docked in New York City in a thunder-storm.

There were thousands of people waiting on the pier.

But the first person George saw as they walked down the gangplank was Papa. He rushed up to George and Phoebe, grabbing them both and pulling them to him. All around them, people cried with happiness. Others just cried, their tears mixing with the pouring rain.

They introduced Papa to Marco and Enzo, but there wasn't much time to talk. Their train to

Millerstown was leaving soon, and an ambulance was waiting to take Marco to the hospital.

Luckily, George didn't have to say a real good-bye to Marco and Enzo.

Aunt Daisy was staying in New York City to take care of Enzo until Marco's feet were healed. And then they would come with her for a visit to Millerstown. Seeing the way Marco and Aunt Daisy were looking at each other, George wondered if maybe Marco and Enzo would stay forever. George sure hoped so.

As they rode to the train station, newsboys screamed from every street corner.

"Read all about it! Titanic survivors in New York! More than fifteen hundred people dead! Read all about it!"

George covered his ears.

He wanted to forget everything about the *Titanic*.

He wanted to put it out of his mind forever.

CHAPTER 16

But he couldn't forget.

Even back on the farm, surrounded by friends from school and neighbors from town, he felt like he was still drifting on the dark ocean. And each day that went by, he felt himself drifting farther away. At night, when he got into bed, he'd see the faces of all those scared people on G deck. He'd see the ship disappearing into the sea. He'd remember the stabbing cold, and the screams of hundreds of people crying for help.

He didn't bother trying to fall asleep. Each night, after Phoebe and Papa were in bed, he went out into the woods.

He was heading back to the house one night when he heard a noise through the bushes.

Something was there. He could sense it.

The panther?

He took out his knife, fighting the urge to run away, and peered through the branches.

George stared in shock.

It was Papa.

He was sitting on a large rock, looking up at the sky, smoking his pipe. He looked like he'd been there for some time.

Papa turned. He didn't look especially surprised to see George.

"Sorry to give you a scare," he said.

"What are you doing here?" George asked.

"Don't know," Papa said. "Sometimes I just come here, when I can't sleep."

George couldn't believe it. How many nights

had they both been out in the woods at the same time?

Papa eased himself off the rock and began walking back toward the house. "I'll take you up to your bed."

"No, Papa," George said. "I come to the woods too."

Papa looked at him with a very slight smile.

"I know that," he said.

Papa knew? What else did Papa know about George?

What else *didn't* George know about Papa?

He and his father looked at each other. Really looked, for the first time in a long while, maybe since Mama died.

Suddenly George started to cry. They took him by surprise, his tears, and he couldn't stop. He cried for all those people who didn't make it out of the water. He cried because somehow he did. He cried because he knew that no matter how

94

much time went by, a part of him would still be out in that ocean. He would never forget.

Papa held George's hand and didn't say a word. And then he led George over to the boulder, where they sat together under the stars.

George stared up at the sky. Were those really the same stars that had burned so brightly above the black ocean that night?

Was he really still the same boy?

George, who couldn't stay out of trouble. George, who didn't try hard at school.

George, who found the escape ladders. George, who pulled Marco to that lifeboat.

Who didn't give up.

They sat on the boulder for a long while, and as the sun started to peep over the trees, George told Papa about Mr. Andrews.

"He said he thought one day I'd build a ship."

Papa didn't laugh. He puffed on his pipe, looking thoughtful.

"How about we build one together?" Papa said. "A nice little boat. For the pond. I've always wanted to do that."

"That's a good idea," George said.

A great idea.

"We could start today," Papa said, standing up and holding out his hand.

They walked back to the house together. The birds were singing softly. The chickens were squawking for breakfast. A breeze was whispering through the trees. And a voice seemed to sing to George, very softly:

> *"Awake, awake.*
> *It's now daybreak!*
> *But don't forget your dreams. . . ."*

Papa looked out into the woods, like he could hear it too.

MY *TITANIC* STORY

This book is a work of historical fiction. That means that all of the facts about the *Titanic* are true, but the main characters came from my imagination. George, Phoebe, Aunt Daisy, Marco, and Enzo are based on people I learned about while researching the *Titanic*. By the time I finished writing this book, they sure felt real to me.

I can see George now, relaxing in the little boat he and Papa built, rowing around their pond while Phoebe watches from the shore, reading a book about dinosaur fossils. I can picture Aunt Daisy and Marco's wedding, how Enzo would run down the aisle with a huge grin on his face. That's my favorite part of being a writer, giving my characters happiness in the end. If only I could do the same for the 1,517 people who didn't survive the sinking of the *Titanic*.

What a sad and terrible story!

One day as I was trying to finish the book, I needed a break, so I went to New York City with my eleven-year-old son, Dylan. We stopped to rest in one of my favorite neighborhoods, in a tiny park on West 106th Street and Broadway with trees and a bronze statue of a woman lying on her side. I read the gold writing engraved in a marble bench, and to my surprise I saw that the entire park was a memorial to two famous New Yorkers who died on the *Titanic*, Isidor and Ida Straus.

I couldn't forget the *Titanic*, it seemed, not even for an afternoon.

And nearly one hundred years later, the world hasn't forgotten either.

FACTS ABOUT THE *TITANIC*

More has been written about the *Titanic* than any other disaster in modern history. I tried to include as much information as I could in the book. But here are some more amazing facts that I wanted to share with you.

- The *Titanic* was the largest ship—the largest moving object—ever built. It weighed close to 50,000 tons, and was eleven stories tall and four city blocks long.

- There were 2,229 people on board—1,316 passengers and 913 crew. Survivors included 498 passengers and 215 members of the crew.

- The passengers came from 28 different countries, including many from America, England, Ireland, and

Finland. There were a few passengers from China, Japan, Mexico, and South Africa. Most of the crew members were from England and Ireland.

- There were nine dogs on the *Titanic*. They stayed in kennels, but their owners could take them out onto the decks for walks. Two Pomeranians and one Pekingese survived with their masters.

- After the sinking of the *Titanic*, laws were changed to require all ships to carry enough lifeboats for every passenger and crew member.

- For decades, divers, scientists, and treasure hunters searched for the wreck of the *Titanic*. It was finally located in 1985 by a team led by U.S. scientist Robert Ballard, 2 1/2 miles below the surface of the sea.

- Ballard and his team did not take anything from the wreck. Dr. Ballard believes the *Titanic* should rest in peace as a memorial to those who died. But he couldn't stop treasure hunters from diving to the wreck and removing thousands of artifacts: jewelry, dishes, clothes, even the ship's hull.

What do you think about this? Do you think the *Titanic* should be brought to the surface or left in peace?

**Can you survive another thrilling
story based on true events?**

Read on for a sneak peek at

I SURVIVED

THE SHARK ATTACKS
OF 1916

Ten-year-old Chet and his best friends, Dewey
and T.J., rushed down the path toward the creek.
It was the hottest day anyone could remember in
their little town of Springville, New Jersey. So hot
Papa actually let Chet leave work early to take a
swim at the creek.

They stripped off their clothes and raced to the
dock. Chet was the first to leap into the air and
cannonball into the creek.

Dewey splashed down right after, with T.J. just behind.

"Chet! Catch!" T.J. said, sending his rubber ball through the air.

Chet leaped up and caught it, then turned to throw to T.J. But T.J. was looking down the creek. His eyes were so strange that Chet almost dropped the ball. T.J. looked terrified.

"What's wrong?" Chet said, looking all around.

Last summer a snapping turtle had almost bitten off Dewey's finger. There were also snakes, a few mean enough to bite you if you got too close.

But T.J. was looking at something else. Something Chet had never seen before. A black triangle sticking up through the water.

Could it be . . . was that a shark's fin?

No, Chet thought, shaking his head. It couldn't be. His eyes were playing tricks on him. His mind was messed up because of those shark attacks down at the shore, those two men attacked while they were swimming. The blood. The ladies fainting on the beach. No wonder they were seeing sharks in the creek.

There couldn't be a shark in the creek. That was crazy. Chet tried to laugh, but T.J. was still standing there with that terrified look, and now Dewey was rushing through the water toward the grass.

"Get out of the water!" he yelled.

The black triangle was coming right at them, faster, faster, closer, closer.

Chet swam as fast as he could, but T.J. just stood there, frozen. "T.J.!" Chet shouted. "Hurry!"

But it was too late. The shark was heading right for T.J., and he screamed.

There was a huge splash.

And then he was gone.